Jessica Potter

P9-DMO-051

Clouds and Clocks

Story copyright © 1989 by Matthew R. Galvin.
Note to Parents and illustrations copyright © 2007 by Magination Press.
All rights reserved. Except as permitted under the
United States Copyright Act of 1976,
no part of this publication may be reproduced or distributed in
any form or by any means, or stored in a database or retrieval system,
without the prior written permission of the publisher.

Published by
MAGINATION PRESS
An Educational Publishing Foundation Book
American Psychological Association
750 First Street, NE
Washington, DC 20002

For more information about our books, including a complete catalog,
please write to us, call 1-800-374-2721,
or visit our website at www.maginationpress.com.

The text type is Bookman
Editor: Darcie Conner Johnston
Art Director: Susan K. White
Printed by Worzalla, Stevens Point, Wisconsin

Library of Congress Cataloging-in-Publication Data

Galvin, Matthew.
Clouds and clocks : a story for children who soil /
written by Matthew Galvin ; illustrated by M.S. Weber. — 2nd ed.
        p.   cm.
Summary: When circumstances in his life become upsetting, Andrew stops
using the toilet. Includes a Note to Parents about soiling.
ISBN-13: 978-1-59147-733-4 (hardcover : alk. paper)
ISBN-10: 1-59147-733-6 (hardcover : alk. paper)
ISBN-13: 978-1-59147-734-1 (pbk. : alk. paper)
ISBN-10: 1-59147-734-4 (pbk. : alk. paper)
1. Encopresis—Juvenile literature. 2. Constipation in children—
Juvenile literature. 3. Enuresis—Juvenile literature.
I. Weber, M. S. (Michael S). II. Title.
RJ506.E5G35 2007
618.92'849—dc22   2006037529

10 9 8 7 6 5 4 3 2 1

Clouds and Clocks

A STORY FOR CHILDREN WHO SOIL
SECOND EDITION

written by Matthew Galvin, M.D.

illustrated by M.S. Weber

MAGINATION PRESS • WASHINGTON, DC

Andrew liked spending time with his grandfather. The two of them often sat on the porch, relaxing and looking up at the sky. They played a game of finding just the right names for different kinds of clouds. "That's a chalk-dust sky," Granddad might say. "Chalk-dust clouds on a blue chalkboard."

Clouds made them think of many different things. Andrew saw castles and dinosaurs and herds of buffalo. A sky of swirling gray and white reminded Granddad of an oyster shell. Sometimes they could see a treasure map of shifting continents and islands.

"Andy, look over there," said Granddad. "What would you call that?"

Andrew looked up at thin streaks of clouds with blue sky between them. "Tiger stripes!" he said.

Andrew and his mother lived with Granddad.
Andrew's father died when Andrew was a baby.

"Your dad left you something to remember him by,"
Granddad told him.

It was his dad's watch. Andrew was very proud
to have it, but he didn't know how to tell time.
Grandad said, "You'll learn someday soon."

Andrew's mother worked all day and went to school at night. Often Andrew was in bed before she came home. Other nights she spent all her time on schoolwork. Andrew was sad that his mother worked so much, but he liked being with his grandfather.

But Granddad started to seem different.
He said he didn't feel good. And he spent
more time alone in his room. Andrew
didn't know why, and he was worried.
He didn't want to go to school and leave
Granddad all alone. But his mother said
he couldn't stay home.

Every morning when Andrew ate breakfast,
his mother said, "Hurry or you'll be late."
Then she told him to use the bathroom.

"I don't have to," Andrew always said.
But when they were in the car, he changed
his mind. His mother often got mad. But
she got him to school on time.

One day after school,
Andrew's mother said,
"Granddad isn't feeling well.
He is going to the hospital."

"Why?" asked Andrew,
trying hard not to cry.

"So the doctors can find out
what the problem is,"
said Granddad, giving him a hug.
"I'll be back soon, Andy."

Then Andrew began having a problem of his own. It happened in school the next day. He didn't want to use the bathroom there. After a while Andrew went to the bathroom in his pants.

One of the kids shouted, "Andrew pooped in his pants!" Others teased him and called him stinky. Andrew's teacher called it an accident and took him to the bathroom to clean up. "Everyone has an accident now and then," she said. Andrew promised to try to use the toilet in time.

Andrew tried to keep his promise, but his problem didn't get any better. Instead, it got worse. He didn't even use the bathroom at home when he should. His mother was mad at him a lot, especially when she found the underpants full of poop that he had hidden under his bed.

"Andrew, why are you doing this?" she asked.

Andrew didn't say anything.
He didn't even want to think about it.
But he didn't like having his mom mad at him.

Finally, Andrew and his mother went to see Dr. Henry. Mom told Dr. Henry about Andrew's problem. Andrew wanted to hide. When Dr. Henry said, "I know many kids your age who have the same problem," Andrew was really surprised.

Dr. Henry asked Andrew if he wanted to find a way to solve the problem. "Yes," Andrew almost whispered.

"First of all," said Dr. Henry, "I'll need to check your bottom, just like I check your ears and throat."

After that, Dr. Henry explained, "Andy, your problem is called soiling. I'll give you one kind of medicine to clean your insides, then a medicine called mineral oil to take at breakfast time and again at dinner. You also need to sit on the toilet for ten minutes after breakfast and ten minutes after dinner to let the medicine work."

"Do I have to go to the hospital?" Andrew wondered.

"No," said Dr. Henry, "but I would like you and your mother to see another doctor, one who talks with and listens to children. Her name is Dr. Rachel."

In Dr. Rachel's office, there was a round table with paper and lots of crayons. Dr. Rachel asked Andrew, "Can you tell me about your problem?"

Andrew felt embarrassed. "It's called soiling," he said. Then he added, "It's fixed now."

Dr. Rachel said, "I'm glad about that."

"I don't want to talk about it any more," Andrew told her.

"Okay," said Dr. Rachel. "Let's draw some pictures instead."

Andrew liked to draw. He drew a picture of his family at home. In the sky above the house, Andrew drew a dark whirling cloud. Dr. Rachel said, "That tornado looks scary."

Andrew nodded. Then he pointed to the man in the picture. "This is my Granddad," he said, "but he isn't home right now."

"Oh?" said Dr. Rachel. "Where is he?"

Andrew looked down. "In the hospital," he said softly.

"Tell me about your Granddad," suggested Dr. Rachel.

"I miss him," Andrew said, crying a little.

Andrew told Dr. Rachel about the cloud game
he played with Granddad. Then Dr. Rachel asked
about Andrew's mother.

"She's very busy," Andrew said. He didn't feel
like talking about her. "I have a watch," he told
Dr. Rachel, "but I can't tell time."

"You'll learn one day soon, Andy," Dr. Rachel said
with a smile. "You know, your body can tell time."
Andrew was surprised. "Your body can tell you when
it's time to use the bathroom," explained Dr. Rachel.

"You mean like a clock?" asked Andrew.

"Sort of," replied Dr. Rachel.
"We'll talk more about it next time."

But the next time Andrew saw Dr. Rachel, he didn't want to talk about his body. He had been taking the medicine, but he was still having accidents. He wouldn't even look at her.

"I hate school!" he said at last.

"What do you hate about it?" asked Dr. Rachel.

"All the kids tease me all the time," Andrew told her.

"Sometimes that happens when a person soils," she said. "But it won't go on forever, especially when you've solved the problem."

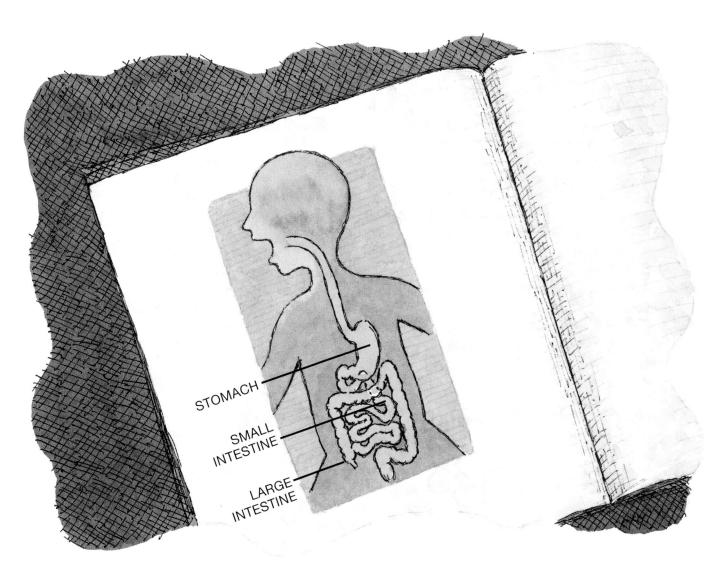

STOMACH

SMALL
INTESTINE

LARGE
INTESTINE

Dr. Rachel showed Andrew a drawing.
It showed how a person's stomach is connected
to a long, curving tube called the small intestine
and a bigger tube called the large intestine.
"The big tube is open at the bottom," she told him.

"Is that where the poop comes out?" asked Andrew.

"Right," said Dr. Rachel. "Your intestine is a special
tube. It can tell when it's full of poop. It sends a
message to your brain that it's time to use the toilet."

Andrew said, "But sometimes when I go to the bathroom nothing comes out, even when I push hard."

Dr. Rachel said, "When a person has stopped listening to his body for a while, sometimes the tube gets too full of poop. It stops sending messages to the brain."

Andrew thought for a minute. "Does that mean the clock in the body doesn't tell the right time any more?" he asked.

"It's not a real clock like your watch," said Dr. Rachel, "but that's the idea."

"How do you fix it?" asked Andrew.

Dr. Rachel said, "The mineral oil makes it work more smoothly. It lets the poop come out when you sit on the toilet. But you can help by relaxing."

"What's relaxing?" Andrew wanted to know.

"Relaxing," explained Dr. Rachel, "is when you let your body feel very good inside. You can use your imagination to help you." Dr. Rachel asked Andrew to remember a time when he felt very good inside.

Andrew thought about playing the cloud game with Granddad. He smiled. "I'm thinking about clouds," he told Dr. Rachel.

"Good," she said. "Now imagine a sky full of your favorite colors and beautiful clouds."

Andrew closed his eyes to imagine better.
In his mind the clouds changed shape and drifted by.

"You can drift with the clouds, feeling very good inside, if you like," he heard Dr. Rachel say.

When Andrew opened his eyes, he did feel very good inside.

"There are all kinds of times you can use your imagination to relax," Dr. Rachel said.

"Like when I have to sit on the toilet after breakfast and dinner?" asked Andrew.

Dr. Rachel smiled. "If you like. It doesn't take a lot of time to relax." Then she said, "Let's ask your mother to come in. We'll tell her what we've been doing."

During the next few weeks, some good things began to happen. Andrew learned to relax. Andrew's mother told him that he was doing a good job using the bathroom on time after breakfast and after dinner.

Sometimes she forgot the mineral oil and he reminded her. After a while he began to think that she needed to learn to relax, too. Andrew told her about using her imagination. He and his mom both began to spend time relaxing. Pretty soon he stopped soiling.

The kids at school didn't tease Andrew much any more. He made some new friends. One friend's father studied the weather. He came to school to talk about it. Andrew was excited, especially when they learned about clouds. School was a good place to learn about all kinds of things. Andrew even began to learn how to tell time.

The very best thing that happened, though, was that Granddad came home from the hospital. He told Andrew that he had to take some medicine, too.

"Are you feeling better now?" Andrew asked.

Granddad said, "Yes, I am. The medicine and talking to the doctor help."

After that, they went for a walk together.

NOTE TO PARENTS

by Virginia Shiller, Ph.D.

Soiling is the common term used to describe the depositing of stools in inappropriate places, such as underwear or pajamas. When a child has a problem with soiling, it is usually embarrassing, frustrating, and isolating for him or her, especially when it occurs around peers. Moreover, it is generally a very disturbing symptom for parents, siblings, and other family members. While not highly common, studies show that one or two children in a hundred have the symptom of soiling (or in technical terms, encopresis), and that boys are three to four times more likely than girls to soil.

PHYSICAL AND EMOTIONAL CAUSES

Parents may be tempted to view the child who soils as lazy or willful, and to think that lecturing or scolding will correct the problem. However, this is a behavior that can have both physical and psychological roots, and an understanding of the underlying factors for any particular child is important in figuring out how to solve the problem.

Often the cause is primarily physical. For example, a child who has had normal bowel movements may experience an episode of constipation resulting from a diet change, illness, or anxiety about using unfamiliar toilets when traveling or attending camp. A vicious cycle may then occur when the child becomes afraid of passing a hard stool and holds back to avoid pain. If this pattern continues over time, retained stools can cause changes in the colon muscles. Stretched-out, flabby muscles are less able to push large, hard stools out, nor can they hold liquid that leaks from around the hard mass. The result is leakage, often occurring without the child's awareness.

Other times, the cause for soiling is mainly in the emotional realm. Anxiety can affect the body in a variety of ways, and one way is through tension in the colon. Anxiety can cause constipation, followed by the events just discussed. It can also make children feel less in control of their lives, and lack of control of bowel movements can be the outward physical sign that a child is struggling emotionally.

Sometimes, when children experience anxiety about events in their life that are beyond their control, they may without quite realizing it begin to seek more control in arenas where control is possible. Bathroom events are a big part of a young child's life, so they can easily become the focus of children's emotional concerns. When children have an obstinate streak, this may confound the problem, with children expressing their tendency to be oppositional by determining when and where they defecate.

When the problem has a basis that is primarily physical, treatment by a pediatrician may be sufficient to cure the problem. Other times, when soiling reflects emotional concerns, teamwork between a physician and a therapist is necessary to solve the difficulty.

HOW THIS BOOK CAN HELP

Clouds and Clocks describes one child's struggle with soiling. Since each child who soils is likely to have unique experiences contributing to the symptom and may need a slightly different approach to treatment, the story will not be a perfect fit for every child.

However, most children will be able to identify with at least some of the experiences of Andrew, the boy in this story. In hearing of his struggle, children will feel less alone and less confused about a symptom that often makes them the target of cruel remarks from peers. The book can also help children understand the rationale for common treatments, such as taking mineral oil to make stools easier to pass.

When you read *Clouds and Clocks* with your child, you can enhance its usefulness in the following ways:

- **Talk About Stressful Events**

  If your child has experienced stressful events in his or her life that coincided with the beginning of soiling, then Andrew's anxiety about his grandfather's hospitalization can provide an avenue to discussing the unique stressors in your child's life. Casually commenting "Gee, that's a little bit like when Daddy and I were arguing a lot, and Daddy moved to his new house" can help your child gain understanding about how his own fears and worries may be related to the soiling problem. Some children may just nod, but others may open up and express thoughts they have not previously shared.

- **Learn About the Digestive System**

  As you read the section in which Andrew's therapist provides him with a diagram of the digestive system, you may want to pause and ask your child if he or she is surprised by this information or has questions about it. Children typically have little idea about what happens to food between the time they swallow it and when stools emerge. Understanding more about the insides of their body can help children who feel powerless gain more of a sense of control and mastery.

- **Focus on Relevant Information**

  You may want to emphasize the aspects of the story that are most relevant to your child's problem. If your child's encopresis seems to have a basis that is primarily physical, then the information about appropriate medications and the importance of establishing regular times to sit on the toilet may be most helpful. When a physical problem has become compounded by anxiety, then the relaxation exercises can provide critical assistance to allow the other aspects of the plan to work.

- **Consider Relaxation Exercises**

  If your child is interested in trying relaxation exercises, you may want to guide him or her in choosing an imaginative scenario that will bring forth positive memories plus encourage a sense of being in charge. In *Clouds and Clocks*, the cloud scenes that Andrew imagines provide him with a rewarding link to happy times with his grandfather. Most likely, Andrew also feels empowered by being able to be the master of the cloud designs.

This book may be used as a self-help measure, along with the guidance of your pediatrician, or it can be an adjunct to work with a therapist. If use of the book on your own does not result in positive changes, then a consultation with a psychologist or other mental health specialist is advised. In some cases, encopresis may result from a complex interaction of factors, and it may take time and specialized knowledge to solve the problem.

Virginia Shiller, Ph.D., is a clinical psychologist specializing in child and family therapy. She maintains a private practice in New Haven, Connecticut, and is the author, with Meg Schneider, of Rewards for Kids! Ready-to-Use Charts and Activities for Positive Parenting.

ABOUT THE AUTHOR

MATTHEW GALVIN, M.D., is a psychiatrist with an expertise in children and adolescents, as well as the author of several books on topics of special concern to young people, including *Otto Learns About His Medicine: A Story About Medication for Children with ADHD.* He lives with his family in Indiana.

ABOUT THE ILLUSTRATOR

M.S. (MICHAEL) WEBER is a graduate of the Art Institute of Chicago. His illustrations appear in children's magazines and books, and online at Magickeys.com. "I look upon children as a new frontier," he says, "because if children are well influenced through their parents, education, and literature, the chances of our world becoming a better place will improve. This is why I illustrate children's stories." He lives in Chicago with his family.